MY PARENTS WON'T STOP TALKING!

BLAH BLAH
Blahblah BLAH **BLAH**
BLAH BLAH BLAH
BLAH

Emma Hunsinger

Tillie Walden

Roaring Brook Press

New York

Emma Hunsinger dedicates her half of this book to Tillie Walden.
Tillie Walden dedicates her half of this book to Emma Hunsinger.

Published by Roaring Brook Press • Roaring Brook Press is a division of Holtzbrinck
Publishing Holdings Limited Partnership • 120 Broadway, New York, NY 10271 • mackids.com

Library of Congress Cataloging-in-Publication Data is available. • ISBN 978-1-250-80027-5

Our books may be purchased in bulk for promotional, educational, or business use.
Please contact your local bookseller or the Macmillan Corporate and Premium Sales Department
at (800) 221-7945 ext. 5442 or by email at MacmillanSpecialMarkets@macmillan.com.

First edition, 2022 • Book design by Sharismar Rodriguez • The illustrations for this book were created on large pieces
of watercolor paper and drawn with Blackwing Pencils. Those drawings were then scanned and colored on an iPad in
Procreate. Emma drew the characters and Tillie drew the backgrounds, and they worked on the coloring together.

Printed in China by RR Donnelley Asia Printing Solutions Ltd., Dongguan City, Guangdong Province

10 9 8 7 6 5 4 3 2 1

I can't wait to go to the park!

I'm going to bake and
sell mud pies.

I'm going to run between
the people swinging.

Ex-squeeze
me.

And I'm going
to climb my
favorite tree.

Finally, everyone's ready!

I can't wait to go to the park.

My mom likes to listen to
meditation podcasts.

My other mom likes to walk around
and think really hard.

My brother, Seth, likes to
put sand back in
the sandbox.

05/2022

I like to—

Oh no.

But it's OK—
I've waited before.

I'm amazing at waiting.

No one waits better than me. No one.

I know I can wait because every day in school, we line up in alphabetical order, and I'm always at the end.
(My last name is Zurowski.)

One time I even waited a whole hour after my piano lesson because my parents got stuck in traffic and I had to sit with Mrs. Gruyere while she folded laundry.

and then sit through 35 of Seth's
boring ballet recitals

and then drive there and back to Grandma's house
in Florida 67 times with only rice cakes to eat,
and I wouldn't mind at all.

OK. I can do this.
I can wait.

I'm just gonna do some
normal waiting things.
Like tapping my foot

and fixing
my sock

and biting my
fingernails

and groaning loud enough
that my moms can hear but not
loud enough that they tell me to
stop being rude.

When I talk to my friends, we talk about interesting things, like what we would do if the world was made of food and how our houses could be doughnuts and cars would be pizzas and gummy bears would be actual bears.

Grown-ups only talk about boring things, like driving to the mall to return something and work phone calls and how much they like cooking vegetables and all the people they know who I've never met!

Like JD, or Stephanie, or Mary Taylor, or Jim S. Or Jim T. Or Anita Hernandez, or Whatsherface Murchison, or Ellen Somethingorother, or Tommy Sneakers, or Thorton Torango,

or Salazar Saladbar, or Dr. Doody, or Cucumberto Pepino, or James McJames, or Domingo Dodecagon, or Geminor Ronkonkoma, or Oliver G. Crabcakers.

I will not stand for this.

They must stop talking.

I've done all I can.

But instead I'm here.

Seth clearly doesn't
understand how bad it is.

He's too young to
understand it's hopeless.

I give up.

forever.

In forever, there is nothing.
No park. No parents. No Credenzas.
No waiting.

No anything.

Only me.

I know what I need to do.

I need to be my own slide.

I need to be my own water fountain
that shoots out super high.

I need to be my own
pet chipmunk.

I need to become my own park.